Hattie and the Fox

by Mem Fox
Illustrated by Patricia Mullins

Aladdin Paperbacks
New York London Toronto Sydney

Hattie was a big black hen.
One morning she looked up and said,
'Goodness gracious me!
I can see a nose in the bushes!"

"Good grief!" said the goose.
"Well, well!" said the pig.

"Who cares?" said the sheep.
"So what?" said the horse.
"What next?" said the cow.

And Hattie said,
"Goodness gracious me!
I can see a nose
and two eyes in the bushes!"

"Good grief!" said the goose.
"Well, well!" said the pig.
"Who cares?" said the sheep.
"So what?" said the horse.
"What next?" said the cow.

And Hattie said,
"Goodness gracious me!
I can see a nose, two eyes,
and two ears in the bushes!"

"Good grief!" said the goose.
"Well, well!" said the pig.
"Who cares?" said the sheep.
"So what?" said the horse.
"What next?" said the cow.

And Hattie said,
"Goodness gracious me!
I can see a nose, two eyes, two ears,
and two legs in the bushes!"

"Good grief!" said the goose.
"Well, well!" said the pig.
"Who cares?" said the sheep.
"So what?" said the horse.
"What next?" said the cow.

And Hattie said,
"Goodness gracious me!
I can see a nose, two eyes, two ears, two legs,
and a body in the bushes!"

"Good grief!" said the goose.
"Well, well!" said the pig.
"Who cares?" said the sheep.
"So what?" said the horse.
"What next?" said the cow.

And Hattie said,
"Goodness gracious me!
I can see a nose, two eyes, two ears, a body, four legs,
and a tail in the bushes!
It's a fox! It's a fox!"
And she flew very quickly into a nearby tree.

"Oh, no!" said the goose.
"Dear me!" said the pig.
"Oh, dear!" said the sheep.
"Oh, help!" said the horse.

But the cow said, "MOO!"

so loudly that the fox was frightened and ran away.

And they were all so surprised
that none of them said anything
for a very long time.

ALADDIN PAPERBACKS
An imprint of Simon & Schuster Children's Publishing Division
1230 Avenue of the Americas, New York, NY 10020
Text copyright © 1986 by Mem Fox
Illustrations copyright © 1986 by Patricia Mullins
All rights reserved, including the right of reproduction
in whole or in part in any form.
ALADDIN PAPERBACKS and colophon are registered
trademarks of Simon & Schuster, Inc.
Also available in a Simon & Schuster Books for Young Readers hardcover edition.
Manufactured in the United States of America
First Aladdin Paperbacks edition 1992
This Aladdin Paperbacks edition June 2005
10 9 8 7 6 5 4 3 2 1
The Library of Congress has cataloged the hardcover edition as follows:
Fox, Mem, 1946-
Hattie and the fox / by Mem Fox ; illustrations by Patricia Mullins.
p. cm.
Summary: Hattie, a big black hen, discovers a fox in the bushes,
which creates varying reactions in the other barnyard animals.
ISBN 0-02-735470-9 (hc.)
[1. Chickens—Fiction. 2. Foxes—Fiction. Domestic animals—Fiction]
I. Mullins, Patricia, 1952- ill.
PZ7.F8373Hat 1992 [E]—dc20 86-18849
ISBN 1-4169-0308-9 (pbk.)